Teachers, librarians, and kids from across Canada had an advance look at *Canadian Flyer Adventures* before publication. Here's what some of them had to say:

Great Canadian historical content, excellent illustrations, and superb closing historical facts (I love the kids' commentary!). ~ *SARA S., TEACHER, ONTARIO*

As a teacher–librarian I welcome this series with open arms. It fills the gap for Canadian historical adventures at an early reading level! There's fast action, interesting, believable characters, and great historical information. ~ *MARGARET L., TEACHER–LIBRARIAN, BRITISH COLUMBIA*

The *Canadian Flyer Adventures* will transport young readers to different eras of our past with their appealing topics. Thank goodness there are more artifacts in that old dresser ... they are sure to lead to even more escapades. ~ *SALLY B., TEACHER–LIBRARIAN, MANITOBA*

When I shared the book with a grade 1–2 teacher at my school, she enjoyed the book, noting that her students would find it appealing because of the action-adventure and short chapters. ~ *HEATHER J., TEACHER AND LIBRARIAN, NOVA SCOTIA*

Newly independent readers will fly through each *Canadian Flyer Adventure*, and be asking for the next installment! Children will enjoy the fast-paced narrative, the personalities of the main characters, and the drama of the dangerous situations the children find themselves in. ~ *PAM L., LIBRARIAN, ONTARIO*

I love the fact that these are Canadian adventures—kids should know how exciting Canadian history is. Emily and Matt are regular kids, full of curiosity, and I can see readers relating to them.  ~ *JEAN K., TEACHER, ONTARIO*

## What kids told us:

I would like to have the chance to ride on a magical sled and have adventures.  ~ *EMMANUEL*

I would like to tell the author that her book is amazing, incredible, awesome, and a million times better than any book I've read.  ~ *MARIA*

I would recommend the *Canadian Flyer Adventures* series to other kids so they could learn about Canada too. The book is just the right length and hard to put down.  ~ *PAUL*

The books I usually read are the full-of-fact encyclopedias. This book is full of interesting ideas that simply grab me.  ~ *ELEANOR*

At the end of the book Matt and Emily say they are going on another adventure. I'm very interested in where they are going next!  ~ *ALEX*

I like when Emily and Matt fly into the sky on a sled towards a new adventure. I can't wait for the next book!  ~ *JI SANG*

# Danger, Dinosaurs!

## Frieda Wishinsky

### Illustrated by Dean Griffiths

MAPLE
TREE
PRESS

**Maple Tree Press Inc.**
51 Front Street East, Suite 200, Toronto, Ontario M5E 1B3
www.mapletreepress.com

Text © 2007 Frieda Wishinsky     Illustrations © 2007 Dean Griffiths

Distributed in Canada by Raincoast Books
9050 Shaughnessy Street, Vancouver, British Columbia V6P 6E5

Distributed in the United States by Publishers Group West
1700 Fourth Street, Berkeley, California 94710

**Dedication**
For my son, David, who loved dinosaurs too

**Acknowledgements**
Many thanks to the hard-working Maple Tree team—Sheba Meland, Anne Shone,
Ann Featherstone, Grenfell Featherstone, Deborah Bjorgan, Cali Hoffman, Erin Walker, and
Dawn Todd—for their insightful comments and steadfast support. Special thanks to Dean
Griffiths and Claudia Dávila for their engaging and energetic illustrations and design.

**Cataloguing in Publication Data**
Wishinsky, Frieda
Danger, dinosaurs! / Frieda Wishinsky ; illustrated by Dean Griffiths.

(Canadian flyer adventures ; 2)
ISBN-13: 978-1-897066-81-2 (bound) / ISBN-10: 1-897066-81-3 (bound)
ISBN-13: 978-1-897066-82-9 (pbk.) / ISBN-10: 1-897066-82-1 (pbk.)

1. Dinosaurs—Juvenile fiction. I. Griffiths, Dean, 1967– II. Title.
III. Series: Wishinsky, Frieda. Canadian flyer adventures ; 2.

PS8595.I834D36 2007          jC813'.54          C2006-904141-5

**Design & art direction:** Claudia Dávila
**Illustrations:** Dean Griffiths

We acknowledge the financial support of the Canada Council for the
Arts, the Ontario Arts Council, the Government of Canada through the
Book Publishing Industry Development Program (BPIDP), and the
Government of Ontario through the Ontario Media Development
Corporation's Book Initiative for our publishing activities.

Printed in Canada
Ancient Forest Friendly: Printed on 100% Post-Consumer Recycled Paper

A     B     C     D     E     F

# Contents

# HOW IT ALL BEGAN

Emily and Matt couldn't believe their luck. They discovered an old dresser full of strange objects in the tower of Emily's house. They also found a note from Emily's Great-Aunt Miranda: "The sled is yours. Fly it to wonderful adventures."

When they saw the sled behind the dresser, they sat on it and shimmery gold words appeared:

*Rub the leaf*
*Three times fast.*
*Soon you'll fly*
*To the past.*

The sled rose over Emily's house. It flew over their town of Glenwood. It sailed out of a cloud and into the past. Their adventures on the flying sled had begun! Where will the sled take them next? Turn the page to find out.

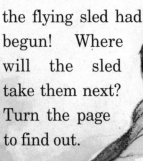

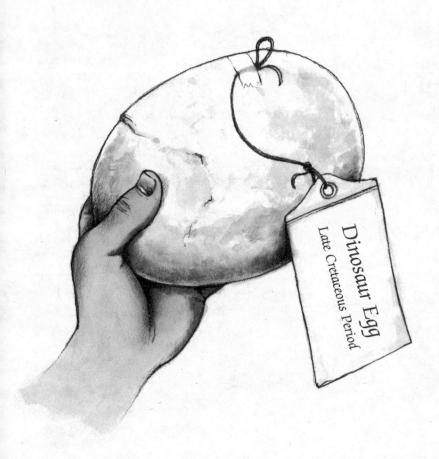

Dinosaur Egg
Late Cretaceous Period

# 1

# The Egg

"My turn!" said Matt. He pulled something large and smooth from the drawer of the mahogany dresser in the tower room. His brown eyes sparkled as he read the tag aloud. "Dinosaur Egg, Late Cretaceous Period!"

"Oh no!" groaned Emily. She knew Matt wanted to have a dinosaur adventure. He loved dinosaurs. He knew everything about them.

"Come on," said Matt. "It will be fun."

"Fun?" said Emily. "Dinosaurs will eat us for lunch."

"Not all dinosaurs," said Matt. "Some dinosaurs like plants, not meat. And anyway, we're smarter than dinosaurs. We'll out-think them."

"But dinosaurs are big. They can squish you."

"Don't worry, Em. Remember those nasty pirates on our first adventure? We came home safely then. Come on! I really want to go."

Emily sighed. "Okay," she said. "We might as well see if the magic will work again."

"Great!" said Matt. "I have my digital recorder in my pocket. I'll describe everything we see, hear, and smell."

"And I have my sketchbook," said Emily. She patted the pocket of her jeans. "I just hope a dinosaur doesn't eat it."

Emily and Matt hopped on the sled. They waited for the magic words to appear.

But nothing happened.

"See. The magic's not working," said Emily. She started to get off the sled.

"Don't go!" shouted Matt, grabbing her arm. "Look!"

Shimmery gold words began to form around the maple leaf painted on the front of the sled.

*Rub the leaf*
*Three times fast.*
*Soon you'll fly*
*To the past.*

"Yahoo!" shouted Matt. "The magic is back. It's going to work!"

Emily sighed and sat back on the sled.

Matt rubbed the leaf three times quickly.

Immediately, a thick fog surrounded them.

It was just like on their first adventure. They couldn't see anything. Then the fog cleared.

They were no longer in Emily's tower.

They were no longer in Emily's house.

They were no longer in the town of Glenwood.

"We're flying!" sang Matt.

The sled flew into a thick, white cloud. Soon it sailed out of the cloud and over a dark forest. Beside it lay a large swamp surrounded by high wavy grass.

The sled turned and flew over a flat plain. Then it headed down toward a small, rocky hill.

"Here we go!" shouted Matt. They held on tightly to the sides of the sled. With a soft thump, the sled landed on a muddy patch on the hill.

Matt and Emily hopped over the mud.

They peered around. There were rocks and boulders everywhere. Some dotted the hillside. Others lay at the bottom of the hill.

"Do you see any dinosaurs?" asked Emily.

"No, but I see giant footprints." Matt pointed to the muddy ground near the sled.

Emily gulped. The footprints were huge and fresh. No animal she'd ever seen could take steps that big.

Matt's eyes glittered with excitement.

"Awesome! They must be dinosaur footprints," he said. "We're in dinosaur times, all right. We'll be the first humans to see real, live dinosaurs!"

"Or the first humans to be eaten by real, live dinosaurs," said Emily.

"We won't be eaten. The sled won't let anything bad happen."

"I hope not." Emily glanced at the sled. "The words are gone."

"They'll come back just like they did last time. Come on, Em. Let's explore the hill."

# 2

# Breaking News!

"Let's hide the sled there," said Emily. She pointed to a small cave carved into a boulder. The boulder was as big as Emily's garage. "We don't want a dinosaur to crush the sled. Then we'd never get back."

Emily and Matt pushed the sled into the cave. They turned to leave.

"Yikes!" screamed Emily. "Look! Over there! It's a… It's a…"

A huge creature stood beside the cave.

"It's amazing!" said Matt.

"It's gigantic," said Emily. "Look at that huge body. Look at that long neck. Look at that big mouth!"

"It's only a Maiasaura. Don't worry. It eats leaves, not girls."

"Are you sure?"

"I'm positive. Is that the face of a meat-eater?"

Emily peered at the Maiasaura. It had a flat head, a broad nose, a spiky crest in front of its eyes, and a bill like a duck. Behind it waddled a smaller Maiasaura. It looked like a giant duckling following its giant mother.

The little Maiasaura waddled up to Emily. It nuzzled her leg like a kitten. It squeaked. "Peep. Peep."

Emily patted it on the head. "It's so cute. I wish I could take it home as a pet. I'd call it Peep, after those funny sounds it makes."

"Imagine what you'd have to do once Peep grew bigger," said Matt.

"We'd probably have to cut a hole in the roof so it could fit. And it would eat so much that we'd have to lug trees home every day to feed it. My dad would complain it was too expensive to keep."

"We'd never be able to keep Peep at my house. My mom hates lizards, so she'd probably hate dinosaurs even more," said Matt.

The little Maiasaura squeaked again. Its mother stared at Emily. Then the little Maiasaura and its mother bent down to chew grass.

Emily pulled out her sketchbook. She drew the little Maiasaura and its mother. Then she sketched a small pile of dinosaur eggs that looked like the egg she and Matt had seen in the dresser. But before she finished her

drawing, the little one stopped eating and pooped!

Matt pulled the recorder out of his pocket. "Breaking News! This is Matt Martinez reporting from dinosaur times. I'm standing beside a mother Maiasaura and her little Maiasaura. The little dinosaur has just pooped. Yes! Ladies and gentlemen, Emily Bing and I are the first humans to see a real, live dinosaur poop!"

"Matt," said Emily. "Who wants to hear that?"

"Everyone. It's awesome."

"It's disgusting," said Emily, holding her nose.

Matt laughed. "Come on, Em. Let's check things out down there near the forest."

Matt and Emily started down the hill. Halfway down, they heard a thumping noise. The thumping grew louder and louder.

"Yikes!" said Matt. "Look!"

A huge creature lumbered out of the forest. It was taller than a three-storey apartment building. It had a giant head, small arms, and a monstrous jaw. It opened its mouth and roared. Emily and Matt could see its spiky, jagged teeth. "It's a... It's a...," stuttered Emily.

"T-t-tyrannosaurus r-r-rex!" stammered Matt. "I can't believe it's so big. Its teeth are as sharp as knives." Matt gulped.

The giant dinosaur roared again. The ground shook like an earthquake.

"I hope it doesn't smell us. T. rex is good at smelling," whispered Matt.

Emily shuddered. "I wish you hadn't said that."

The Tyrannosaurus rex began to walk toward them.

"Quick! Let's run back up!" said Matt.

Emily and Matt raced back up the hill. Part way up, Emily stubbed her toe on the rocks.

"Ow!" she cried.

"Em! It's coming!"

"I can't run fast. I hurt my toe!"

"We have to run fast or we'll be—"

"I'm trying!" cried Emily, hobbling after Matt. "If only we could stop it."

"Quick!" said Matt, pointing to a pile of large rocks at the edge of the hill. Below were even larger rocks. "Let's start a rock slide toward T. rex. If T. rex loses its balance, it might fall."

Emily and Matt grabbed a few large rocks.

"One...two...three...throw!" cried Matt. They threw the rocks down the hill. They pushed bigger and heavier ones. The rocks rolled and smashed into even bigger rocks. Soon, rocks flew like rockets toward T. rex.

The Tyrannosaurus rex roared. It tried to outrun the falling rocks, but it couldn't. T. rex tottered. It roared louder.

Then it stumbled and fell with a deafening thud.

"Run!" shouted Matt.

Emily's toe still ached, but she ran. She could see T. rex moving, struggling to get up.

T. rex slammed its tail against the ground. It roared again and again.

Emily and Matt kept running. They reached the top of the hill. They hid behind a boulder and gasped for air.

Matt peeked down the hill.

"Em, it's up," he whispered. "It's standing. It's walking!"

"Oh no!" cried Emily. "It's coming after us again!"

# 3

# Honk! Honk!

"Honk! Honk!"

"What's that?" asked Emily.

"Honk! Honk! Honk!" The sounds got louder. Closer. A group of large, duck-billed dinosaurs charged out of the forest below.

"It's a herd of Lambeosaurus!" shouted Matt.

The Tyrannosaurus rex saw the herd, too. Its giant teeth gleamed in the sunlight as it turned and lumbered toward them.

Matt and Emily stared as T. rex chased the Lambeosaurus.

The Lambeosaurus fled back toward the forest. The Tyrannosaurus rex roared. It thumped after them.

The Lambeosaurus honked louder and louder. Emily and Matt couldn't keep their eyes off what was happening below. It was like a movie come to life.

"They're warning their friends that there's trouble ahead," said Matt.

"Trouble with a capital T," said Emily.

Matt spoke into his recorder. "Ladies and gentlemen. Emily Bing and I are watching an amazing chase. T. rex is trying to catch a herd of Lambeosaurus. Will he succeed? Will they outrun him? Stay tuned." Matt snapped off his recorder.

"Why are they called Lambeosaurus?" asked Emily. "They don't look like lambs."

"They're named after a Canadian paleontologist called Lawrence Lambe," Matt explained. "Wouldn't it be great to have a dinosaur named after you?"

"How about an Emilysaurus, or a Bingosaurus?" said Emily.

"Or a Mattosaurus," said Matt.

The giant T. rex suddenly roared so loudly, Emily and Matt jumped.

"I bet it's angry that it can't catch those Lambeosaurus," said Matt. "I don't see them anywhere."

"Oh no," said Emily. "Then T. rex will come after us again."

"Look," said Matt. "It's found something it likes even more—over there."

T. rex was bent over a huge, dead dinosaur.

"Wow! It looks like it's enjoying every bite!" said Matt

"I can't look. It's horrible," said Emily. She covered her eyes.

"It would be more horrible if it was chomping on us."

"I don't want to think about that," said Emily.

"Come on, Em. Let's go down the hill the other way—away from the forest."

"Good! Let's get far away," said Emily. "T. rex might still be hungry. And I don't want to be dessert!"

am not. Look up!"

tt peered up. A long creature with a
ail sprinted off a giant oak branch that
the ground. It pulled down another
and chomped on the leaves.

esome," said Matt. "It's a Parksosaurus."

at kind of dinosaur is that? Does it like

laughed. "No. It's named after William
Parks, another Canadian paleontolo-

mall for a dinosaur. And it acts like my
sin, Pete. All Pete does is eat and
ngs, too."

arksosaurus stripped the leaves off
ter branch. It ground the leaves into
its teeth. When it finished chewing,
he bare branches to the ground.

on, Em. Let's keep walking."

# 4

# Cut That Out!

Emily and Matt scurried down the hill away
from the forest.

They walked toward a wide, grassy plain. A
few large trees were grouped together nearby.
It was quiet. The only sounds they could hear
were the hum of insects and their own foot-
steps.

Matt pulled out his recorder. "Matt
Martinez reporting again. The Lambeosaurus
escaped from T. rex, and so did we. But now we
can't see any dinosaurs at all. Where are they?

In the forest? In a lake? In a swamp? Ladies and gentlemen, I ask you. Where are the dinosaurs?"

"Maybe they're taking a nap," said Emily.

Matt snapped off his recorder. "Maybe there are no dinosaurs around here," he said.

"But there are flowers," said Emily. Emily bent over. She sniffed a bunch of small white flowers on a bush.

Matt leaned over a bush covered with small yellow flowers.

"What does your bush smell like?" Emily asked. "This one smells like—ouch!"

Suddenly Emily felt a tree branch knock her over the head. She straightened up. "Cut that out, Matt!"

Matt raised his head up. "Cut what out?"

"You know very well what I'm talking about."

"No, I don't," said Matt.
"You threw a branch at
"I did not. I was checki
"Well if you didn't, wh
"Maybe a branch just
Emily plopped dow
rubbed her head. "Mayb
toe and a sore head.
supposed to hurt."

"It could be worse
be..."

"I know," said Em
smell good here." Em
to sniff the white bus
this. It's like perfum

As Matt knelt
flowers, he was pel

"Em!" he shout
branch. Why are y

"I
Ma
large
lay o
branch
"Aw
"Wh
parks?"
Matt
Arthur
gist."
"It's s
baby cou
throw th
The F
branch a
mush wit
it tossed t
"Come

Matt turned to go. "I can't wait to see what dinosaurs we'll see next."

# 5

# I Want to Go Home!

"I'm hot," said Emily, as they trudged on. "I'm hot and tired. I want to go home."

"But we just got here," said Matt. "There are so many dinosaurs we haven't even seen. There's Triceratops and Ankylosaurus and—"

"I've seen enough dinosaurs. I want to see the rest in movies."

"But this is awesome, Em."

"Maybe to you. But not to me. Besides, if we keep walking, we might get lost and never know how to get back to the sled."

"Well, maybe we should take the sled with us," said Matt.

"Let's check if the magic words are back. Maybe our adventure is over. Maybe it's time to go home."

"I hope not." But Matt knew that was exactly what Emily was hoping would happen.

Matt and Emily climbed back up the hill. The sun beat down on their heads. Sweat poured down their faces.

"Did you hear that?" said Emily. "It sounds like... Look, Matt! It's Peep!"

The little Maiasaura's foot was caught under a big rock. "Peep, peep," it squeaked.

"It's hurt," said Emily. Emily and Matt ran to the rock. They lifted it off the little creature's foot.

"You're free now, Peep," said Matt. "You can go home to your mom." But the little

Maiasaura wouldn't go back to its mother. It nuzzled Matt's leg and peeped.

"It's saying thank you," said Emily, patting its head. "Come on, Matt. Let's find the sled."

"Do you still want to go home? Aren't some dinosaurs cute and friendly?"

"Some dinosaurs are but some are NOT," said Emily as they headed toward the cave. Peep followed them.

"Peep, go home," said Matt. But Peep followed them inside the cave.

"There's the sled," said Matt. "Just where we left it."

"Let's sit on it and see if the magic words appear."

"Come on, Em. I want to stay here a little longer."

"If the magic words appear," said Emily, "we'll know the sled is telling us the adventure is over. Then we'll have to go home. And if it doesn't...well, we can't go home anyway."

Matt sighed. He wished the magic words would not appear. Not now, at least.

Emily sat down on the sled. As Matt hopped on behind her, Peep tried to climb onto the sled.

"You can't come with us, Peep," said Emily. She gave the little dinosaur a gentle shove.

"Peep!" it squeaked. It stood beside the sled as Emily and Matt waited for the magic words. No words appeared.

"Okay. The adventure isn't over," said Matt, jumping off the sled.

"Come on, Matt. You got off too fast. Give the sled a little more time."

"How much time?"

"Let's count up to 100," said Emily. "Then if no words appear, we'll know the adventure isn't over."

Matt popped back on the sled. "One, two, three—" He counted quickly.

"Hey, slow down," said Emily. "You're counting too fast."

# 6

# You Win

"One hundred!" said Matt.

"Okay. You win," said Emily. "The sled wants us to stay."

"So does Peep." The little Maiasaura was still by their side. "You'll see, Em, there are so many fantastic plant-eating dinosaurs."

"And there are so many horrible MEAT-eating dinosaurs," said Emily. She pulled the sled out of the cave. "At least the sled is safe."

Matt spoke into his recorder as Peep followed them out of the cave. "Flash from dinosaur land! Emily and I lifted a rock off a baby dinosaur we called Peep. Now Peep follows us around like a puppy. It—"

Emily tugged at Matt's sleeve. "Come on. Talk into that recorder later. Let's find some water now. I'm so thirsty, I feel like I've been walking in the desert for days."

Matt snapped his recorder off. "There has to be a pond around here somewhere. Dinosaurs have to drink, too."

"Let's go thataway." Emily pointed away from the forest where they had seen T. rex and away from the grassy plain where they'd seen the Parksosaurus.

The children headed down the hill. Peep followed.

"Go home, Peep," said Emily.

The little Maiasaura squeaked and kept following them.

"Your mother won't like it if you come with us," Emily told it.

"It doesn't understand what you're saying," said Matt.

"Peep understands. And, yikes! So does its mom!"

The huge mother Maiasaura was racing toward them.

"She's coming after Peep—and after us!" cried Matt. "I can't believe how fast she's moving."

"Run! She doesn't look friendly!" shouted Emily.

Emily and Matt ran. Peep scurried after them.

"Shoo, Peep. Go home," Matt told the little dinosaur.

But Peep kept following them.

Peep's mother was getting closer and closer.

She smacked the ground furiously with her long, heavy tail.

"She's going to step on the sled!" shouted Emily. "She'll destroy our only way home!"

"She's going to step on us!" shouted Matt. "We're going to be flattened like pancakes! Peep, please GO HOME!"

"Peep! Peep!" squeaked Peep.

But Peep wouldn't go home.

# 7

# Slurp

Emily and Matt raced down the hill.

"Hey," said Matt when they reached the bottom. "I don't hear Peep anymore."

"Me neither," said Emily. Emily and Matt looked up the hill. Peep was nuzzling its mother's giant leg.

Emily flopped down on a soft patch of grass. "Phew! That was close. Plant-eating dinosaurs are dangerous when they're angry."

"Come on, Em. Let's look for a pond. I'm so thirsty, I can't think straight."

Emily stood up. "Your turn to pull the sled," she said.

Matt dragged the sled along an area with tall wavy grass. The sun beat down on their heads, arms, and legs. There were few trees along the way to give them shade.

"There has to be a pond, or a brook, or even a puddle somewhere," said Emily, wiping sweat out of her eyes.

Matt pointed ahead. "I think I see something over there."

"I hope you're right," said Emily. "I'm so thirsty that I could drink a whole pond by myself."

Emily and Matt kept walking.

"It is a pond. I'm sure of it!" cried Matt as they neared the spot he'd seen.

Emily ran toward the pond. Matt followed with the sled. Tall grass encircled the pond.

Emily bent over and cupped the water into her hands. "This is the most delicious water that I've tasted in my whole life," she declared.

Matt slurped a handful. "Awesome!" he said.

Emily sat up and stared at the pond. "It's so hot. I wish we could swim."

"Why can't we?" said Matt. "The pond is shallow. I can see down to the bottom everywhere."

"But we don't have bathing suits."

"Who needs bathing suits? We can swim in our clothes. It's so hot, they'll dry in no time," said Matt.

"So," said Emily.

"So," said Matt.

"So, let's do it!" they said together.

Emily and Matt took off their shoes and socks. Emily took her sketchbook out of her pocket and Matt took his recorder out of his pocket. They placed everything beside the sled on the grass. "It will be hidden and safe here," said Matt.

"One...two...three...in!" they sang.

The water was cool but not icy. The pond was shallow. They could touch bottom everywhere with their feet.

Emily and Matt splashed water at each other.

"This is great," said Matt. "The sky is blue. The water feels good. So, what do you think of dinosaur times now?"

"I...I...think we're not alone," stammered Emily. "I hear something."

Matt looked up. Six huge eyes stared at them. "Yikes! It's three Edmontosaurus!"

Three giant, duck-billed dinosaurs stood beside the pond. They had long, pointed tails, short arms, flat heads, and puffy cheeks.

"What do they eat?" whispered Emily.

"Plants," said Matt.

"Phew," said Emily.

The three dinosaurs were still staring at Emily and Matt.

"Why are they looking at us?" asked Emily. "Do they think we're plants?"

"We don't look like plants. We're not even green. Dinosaurs aren't smart, but they're not that dumb. "

"I wish they'd stop staring," said Emily.

Slowly, one of the Edmontosaurus dipped its long, beak-like snout into the pond. Then it lifted its head and sprayed water all over Matt and Emily.

"Maybe it wants to play," said Matt.

Another Edmontosaurus dipped its snout and sprayed them, too. The third one did the same. Emily and Matt splashed water back at the dinosaurs. The dinosaurs snorted and sprayed them again.

"It's like swimming in a waterfall," said Emily, laughing. "I can't wait to draw a picture of us splashing in a pond with dinosaurs."

"I wish I could tell everyone about this when we get home. But no one would believe me," said Matt.

Just then, one of the Edmontosaurus lifted

its huge foot. It was about to step into the pond. Behind it, the two other Edmontosaurus were about to do the same thing.

"Oh no! We'd better get out of the pond now!" shouted Emily. "There's no room in here for three dinosaurs and us."

# 8

# Smelly Socks

Emily and Matt scrambled out of the pond.

"That was close. Those dinosaurs weren't looking where they were stepping," said Emily. She shook water out of her hair.

"They're just not used to kids. I bet they think we are just two-legged, hairy creatures," said Matt, laughing.

"Luckily we're not two smushed hairy creatures," said Emily. "Come on, Matt. Let's get the sled. Do you see it?"

Together they searched around.

"I can't see it anywhere," said Emily. "I don't see our shoes, or socks, or your recorder, or my sketchbook. What if the Edmontosaurus stepped on everything? What if they smashed the sled?"

"The sled has to be here. If they smashed it, we'd still see pieces of wood," said Matt.

"But what if they ate it? They like leaves. Maybe they like wood, too."

Matt took a deep breath. "The sled is here. I know it is. We just have to look carefully. You go one way and I'll go another. We'll find it. Don't worry, Em."

Matt turned to the right. He walked slowly, feeling the ground through the tall grass. He circled the whole pond. But he found nothing.

Emily turned to the left. She bent over and pushed the grass away. She looked carefully at each clump of grass. When she'd gone completely around, she saw something white.

"I found my sock!" she called.

"Anything else?" asked Matt.

"No. Just one white sock. Oh, Matt. What if that's all that is left? One sock won't take us home."

Emily sank down on the grass. She put her face in her hands.

Matt patted her on the shoulder. "Hey, Em, don't cry."

Emily looked up. "I'm not crying," she said fiercely. "I just wish we hadn't come on this stupid adventure."

"I know the sled is here. It has to be here." Matt took a step to the right. "Yuck!" he screamed. "I stepped in something mushy. It's...dino poop!"

Matt lifted his foot He grabbed an armful of grass and tried to clean the muck off his foot.

Emily laughed.

"It's not funny, Em."

"Yes, it is. Look behind you."

Matt turned. "It's the sled!" he shouted. "Hurray! It's here! And nothing is broken."

"Not even one chip of wood is missing," said Emily.

"But where are our shoes and socks and my recorder and your sketchbook?"

"If one of those Edmontosaurus ate my sketchbook, I hope it has a stomachache," said Emily.

Emily and Matt ran their hands on the ground near the sled.

"Yahoo! Here are my shoes and my recorder. And here's one of my blue socks," said Matt.

"And here are my shoes and my sketchbook!" said Emily. "But not my other white sock. Do you think? No, they couldn't...or could they?"

"They tried," said Matt pointing to the pond.

Two scraps of ripped blue and white fabric floated in the pond.

"I guess dinosaurs don't like the taste of smelly socks," said Emily, laughing.

# 9

# Stuck

"Okay. Now we've seen lots of different dinosaurs," said Emily. "Let's go home."

"Soon," said Matt, washing his feet in the pond. Then he put on his one sock and his shoes. "I still want to see at least one armoured dinosaur—like Ankylosaurus or Triceratops. They're plant-eaters, so they won't eat us. Maybe they'll even have cute little dinosaur babies like Peep."

"Maybe they'll be angry dinosaur mothers like Peep's mother," said Emily. "They might crush us with their pointy tails or pierce us with their sharp bodies. I don't want to be crushed, pierced, smushed, or eaten. I want to go home."

"Well, it's not up to us. If the sled isn't ready to take us home, we can't go."

"Let's check it again," said Emily.

She sat on the sled. Matt hopped on, too.

They waited for the magic words but no words appeared.

"Come on, sled. Take us home," Emily pleaded.

Nothing happened.

Emily rubbed the maple leaf up and down three times.

Nothing.

She rubbed the maple leaf from side to side three times.

Nothing.

She rubbed the leaf hard. She rubbed it soft. No matter which way or how hard or soft she rubbed, nothing happened.

"No fair!" she said. "I want to go home and this sled is not taking us anywhere!"

Emily got off the sled and stomped away.

Matt hurried after her, pulling the sled.

"Slow down, Em!"

Emily didn't answer. She raced ahead. She headed into the high grass. Matt could only see the top of her head.

"Em, wait up! The grass feels different here. It feels squishy."

Emily didn't answer. Matt walked faster. He couldn't even see the top of Emily's head anymore.

Where was she?

"Emily! Emily!" he called. But Emily didn't answer.

Matt began to sweat. His heart pounded. What happened to her?

And then he heard her. She sounded far off.

"Matt! Help!"

"Where are you?" he called back.

"I'm stuck in mud. I can't move. You have to get me out."

"But I can't see you. Keep talking and I'll try and follow the sound of your voice."

"Okay," said Emily. "But, please hurry! I'm sinking. I'm in a swamp."

A swamp! A cold shiver raced up Matt's back. T. rex lived in swamps. Matt had to get Emily out before T. rex showed up.

"Matt! Matt!" Emily called.

Matt tried to follow the sound of her voice.

As he walked, he saw a huge tail not too far off. It looked like a giant club. It was attached to a long, spiky body covered with hard, leathery skin. It was an armoured dinosaur— an Ankylosaurus—and it was grazing on plants in the swamp.

But where was Emily?

"Matt!" she called again.

Her voice was coming from the right.

But he still couldn't see her.

"Matt!" she called again.

Her voice was louder, closer.

And then Matt found her...up to her knees in muck.

## 10

# Hang On

Matt looked for something to pull Emily out of the swamp. But there was nothing around except tall, wavy grass.

Then he saw a large tree. Two thick branches had fallen and lay beside it.

"I'm getting a branch. It will help me pull you out. Hold on, Em. I'll be right back!"

Matt ran to the tree. He tried to lift one of the branches, but it was too heavy. He dragged the branch toward Emily.

"Matt, hurry!" she called.

Matt looked up. The Ankylosaurus was busy eating leaves and grass. But there was something lurking near the Ankylosaurus.

It was big. It was moving. It was—Yikes! It was the Tyrannosaurus rex, and it was coming toward them!

Matt pushed the branch toward Emily. "Can you see the tree branch?" he asked.

"I see it," said Emily.

"Grab it and I'll pull."

Emily grabbed the branch and leaned over it. Matt pulled.

"I'm not moving," said Emily.

He pulled harder.

"Yes! I'm moving now! Well, a bit."

"Are you still stuck?"

"A little."

Matt pulled harder. A terrible roar pierced the air. Matt pulled harder.

"What was that?" asked Emily.

"Nothing. Just hang on."

"I know that roar. It's—"

"Hang on. I'm pulling you out."

Emily held on tightly. Matt pulled as hard as he could.

The Tyrannosaurus rex roared louder.

With one final, hard yank, Matt pulled Emily out of the swamp. "Follow me," he gasped. "We have to get to the sled. Run!"

Emily and Matt raced toward the sled. T. rex roared louder. It was coming closer.

"There's the sled," said Matt. "Hurry! Near that tree."

T. rex lumbered toward the Ankylosaurus. When the Ankylosaurus lifted its head and saw the Tyrannosaurus rex, it stopped eating and roared. It headed toward their tree.

The T. rex roared and stomped after it.

"Quick! Jump on the sled," said Matt. He sat down in front. Emily hopped in behind him. The two dinosaurs were so close now that Matt and Emily could almost smell their breath.

"Come on, sled. Take us home!" yelled Matt.

For a few seconds, nothing happened.

And then, shimmery gold words began to form.

*Rub the leaf*
*Three times fast.*
*It's time to fly*
*Home at last.*

Matt quickly rubbed the maple leaf three times.

They rose in the air. As they soared above the swamp, Emily and Matt stared at T. rex and the Ankylosaurus locked in a fierce and terrible battle.

"Wow!" said Matt, when the sled landed them back at Emily's house. "The sled flew us back just in time."

"And you pulled me out of the swamp just in time," said Emily. "Thanks."

Matt smiled. "Look! My clothes are clean and dry," he said.

"Mine, too. And I have both my white socks," said Emily.

"And I have both my blue ones. That was an awesome adventure."

"It was exciting," Emily agreed. "But it was also horrible. For our next adventure, I want to see people. I don't want to be near anything that wants to step on me or eat me."

"Well, it will be your turn to pick an object for our next adventure."

"I know," said Emily. "And I know just what that will be."

"What?"

"I'll tell you soon," said Emily "Right now, I'm starving. How about a dino dog?"

"What's a dino dog?"

"It's long, juicy, and delicious—especially if you dip it in swamp juice!"

# MORE ABOUT...

After their adventure, Matt and Emily wanted to know more about dinosaurs. Turn the page for their favourite facts.

# Matt's Top Ten Facts

1. Ankylosaurus fought Tyrannosaurus rex by swinging its tail and breaking T. rex's legs.

2. The name "Maiasaura" means "good mother lizard."

3. The name T. rex means "tyrant lizard king."

4. T. rex had about 50 teeth. If one tooth broke off, T. rex could grow another.

Lucky T. rex! It never had to go to the dentist. -E.

5. In 2005, after examining fossilized dinosaur poop, scientists discovered that grass grew at the end of the Cretaceous period. And dinosaurs ate tons of it!

6. From 1906 to 1916, a whole family, the Sternbergs, were dinosaur hunters.

7. The Sternbergs used many tools we use today to hunt for dinosaur fossils. They also used dynamite, which no one uses today because people are afraid it will destroy the fossils.

The Sternbergs used *dino-might!*
-E.

8. The first dinosaur heart found by humans belonged to a plant—eating dinosaur named Thescelosaurus neglectus. It's a reddish—brown fossil, the size of a grapefruit.

9. Two boys, Daniel Helm (age 9) and Mark Turner (age 11) found dinosaur footprints in Britsh Columbia in 2000.

10. Dinosaur Provincial Park and the Royal Tyrrell Museum in Alberta are two of the best places in the world to see dinosaur fossils. In some parts of the park, there are so many you have to be careful not to step on them.

# Emily's Top Ten Facts

**1** Dinosaurs lived on Earth for more than 160 million years.

**2.** Human beings have only lived on Earth for about 200,000 years.

**3.** Dinosaurs have been extinct for about 65 million years.

**4.** Some of the biggest dinosaurs, like plant-eating Apatosaurus, lived in the Jurassic period. Tyrannosaurus rex lived in the Cretaceous period. That's why they never met.

**5.** There was no ice in the Cretaceous period when T. rex roamed around. There was lots of water.

**6.** The first plants with flowers bloomed in the Cretaceous period.

**7.** Scientists have found that duck-billed dinosaurs (like Maiasaura and Lambeosaurus) often had crushed tails. Scientists think that's because they lived in herds and sometimes stepped on each other's tails.

Q: What did the dinosaur say when it stepped on its friend's tail?
A: Iamsosaurus!
—M.

**8.** T. rex's head was more than 1.4 metres (4 1/2 feet) long.

Yikes! That's as big as all of me! —M.

**9.** T. rex was 12.2 metres (40 feet) long.

**10.** There were no flying dinosaurs. The creatures that flew in dinosaur times, called pterosaurs, were flying reptiles.

No flying reptiles allowed

# So You Want to Know...

## From Author Frieda Wishinsky

When I was writing this book, my friends wanted to know more about dinosaurs and the story I wrote. I told them that *Danger, Dinosaurs!* is based on scientific and historical facts. I also told them this:

**What is a fossil?**

A fossil is a remnant, impression, or trace of a plant or animal from long ago, preserved in the Earth's crust.

**What was the Earth like when Tyrannosaurus lived?**

It was a lot like Cathedral Grove on Vancouver Island in Canada. There were lots of ferns and huge trees.

**Why did so many dinosaurs live in what is now called western North America?**

According to paleontologist Philip Currie, many dinosaurs, especially duck-billed and horned ones, liked its cool, mild climate.

**Why are so many dinosaur fossils found in the West?**

The many rivers, lakes, and inland seas in western North America were ideal places for dinosaur bones to become fossils. The glaciers, Badland rivers, and winds all helped create rocks that contain dinosaur fossils.

**When were the first dinosaur bones found?**

People found dinosaur bones many centuries ago but they didn't know what they were. The Chinese thought they were dragon bones. The Europeans thought they were giants' bones or bones of creatures destroyed in the Great Flood mentioned in the Bible.

**Who used the word "dinosaur" first?**

In 1842, Richard Owen, a British paleontologist, called the three large fossil reptiles found in the English countryside "dinosaurs." It was the first time anyone used that word.

**Who discovered the first T. rex?**

In 1884, Canadian Joseph Tyrrell found the first Albertosaurus skull. Albertosaurus is a smaller relative of T. rex. The first T. rex was found in 1902 in Montana.

**How long did a Tyrannosaurus rex live?**

Most lived less than 17 years. If you were 28, you were a very old dinosaur!

**Why didn't a T. rex live longer?**

Many females died of disease. Many males died in nasty fights, often over females.

**Has anyone really found dinosaur poop?**

In 1997, scientist Karen Chin identified a 6.8 kg (15 lb.) fossil, full of bits of smashed bone, as dinosaur poop. It was found beside a dinosaur in Saskatchewan that scientists named Scotty. I bet Karen Chin was glad that fossils don't smell!

**Would you like to see dinosaurs?**

Only in a museum or in the movies!

# Send In Your
# Top Ten Facts

If you enjoyed this adventure as much as Matt
and Emily did, maybe you'd like to collect your own
facts about dinosaurs and paleontology, too.

Email in your favourite facts to
CFATopTen@mapletreepress.com. Maple Tree Press
will choose the very best facts that are sent in to
make a *Canadian Flyer Adventures* Readers' Top Ten
Facts for *Danger, Dinosaurs!*

Each reader who sends in a fact that is selected
for the final Top Ten will receive a new book
in the *Canadian Flyer Adventures* series!
(If more than one person sends in the same fact
and it is chosen, the first person to submit
that fact will be the winner.)

We look forward to hearing from you!

Coming next in the
*Canadian Flyer Adventures* Series…

# Canadian Flyer Adventures
# #3

# Crazy for Gold

Turn the page for a sneak peek.

# From *Crazy for Gold*

Early the next morning, the sun streamed through the cabin's two small windows. Emily woke up and looked around. Everyone was still sound asleep. She slid out of her bedroll, got dressed, and tiptoed outside.

Although the ground was muddy, pink and yellow wildflowers bloomed everywhere. She sat on a damp log and drew a picture of the cabin and a bird in a tree.

"Hi, Em." Matt sat beside her. "What do you want to do now?"

"Look for gold, of course," said Emily.

"But you heard Mr. Langley. There isn't much around."

"We still might find some. I'm good at

finding things. I found my mom's keys after she looked everywhere. Maybe we can find some gold in the stream over there."

"Gold is harder to find than keys," said Matt. "And Mr. Langley panned there already."

"Oh, come on," said Emily. "We still might find something. You never know."

Matt sighed. "Okay. Race you to the stream."

Emily and Matt grabbed a couple of pans by the door and ran to the stream. They made it to the edge at the same time. "Tie!" they sang, laughing. They slipped off their boots and waded into the stream. It was rocky and muddy. They scooped handfuls of sand and swirled it around the pan, peering inside for gold. But there was nothing. Not even a fleck.

"I knew it. Nothing," said Matt.

"Nothing, yet," said Emily.

They scooped some more. Still nothing.

"I'm tired," said Matt. "All this panning is making me hungry. Let's go back."

"Come on," said Emily. "Let's check out one more place over there." She pointed to a small pool of water beside a large rock.

"You check," said Matt. "I'm going back. I bet Mrs. Langley is starting to make breakfast. Maybe she's even baking those scrumptious biscuits."

Matt turned to go.

"Matt!" screamed Emily. "Come here! Look what I've found!"

# The *Canadian Flyer Adventures* Series

## #1 Beware, Pirates!
## #2 Danger, Dinosaurs!

# Upcoming Book

Look out for the next book that will take Emily and Matt on a new adventure:

## #3 Crazy for Gold

And more to come!

# About the Author

Frieda Wishinsky, a former teacher, is an award-winning picture- and chapter-book author, who has written many beloved and bestselling books for children. Frieda enjoys using humour and history in her work, while exploring new ways to tell a story. Her books have earned much critical praise, including a nomination for a Governor General's Award in 1999. In addition to the books in the *Canadian Flyer Adventures* series, Frieda has published *What's the Matter with Albert?*, *A Quest in Time*, and *Manya's Dream* with Maple Tree Press. Frieda lives in Toronto.

# About the Illustrator

Gordon Dean Griffiths realized his love for drawing very early in life. At the age of 12, halfway through a comic book, Dean decided that he wanted to become a comic book artist and spent every spare minute of the next few years perfecting his art. In 1995 Dean illustrated his first children's book, *The Patchwork House*, written by Sally Fitz-Gibbon. Since then he has happily illustrated over a dozen other books for young people and is currently working on several more, including the *Canadian Flyer Adventures* series. Dean lives in Duncan, B.C.